Favorite Greek Myths

BOB BLAISDELL

Illustrated by John Green

DOVER PUBLICATIONS, INC.
New York

DOVER CHILDREN'S THRIFT CLASSICS
EDITOR OF THIS VOLUME: THOMAS CROFTS

Bibliographical Note

Favorite Greek Myths is a new work, first published by Dover Publications, Inc., in 1995.

Library of Congress Cataloging-in-Publication Data

Blaisdell, Robert.
    Favorite Greek myths / Bob Blaisdell ; illustrated by John Green.
       p.   cm. — (Dover children's thrift classics)
    Summary: Retells the stories of the Golden Fleece, the Trojan War, Hercules, and other Greek myths.
    ISBN 0-486-28859-5 (pbk.)
    1. Mythology, Greek—Juvenile literature. [1. Mythology, Greek.] I. Green, John, 1948– ill. II. Title. III. Series.
BL782.B57   1995
292.1'3—dc20   95–30766
                                                          CIP
                                                           AC

Manufactured in the United States of America
Dover Publications, Inc., 31 East 2nd Street, Mineola, N.Y. 11501

Note

THE STORIES from Greek mythology are some of the richest and most vivid in world literature. I have retold the more famous and exciting of the many remarkable tales, basing them on versions by the ancient Greek masters, most notably Homer, Hesiod, Sophocles, Euripides, Apollonius and Apollodorus.

BOB BLAISDELL

Contents

List of Illustrations

Favorite Greek Myths

Chapter I

Gods and Titans

G AIA IS sometimes known as Mother Earth. She is the oldest of all the gods and gives food to every living being. She was created out of Chaos, the swirling formless beginning of all things. By herself Gaia gave birth to Ouranos (the Sky), Ourea (the Mountains) and Oceanus (the Sea).

With her husband Ouranos, she had tremendous children, known as Titans, the Cyclopes and the hundred-handed brutes named Briareus, Gyges and Cottus. Ouranos felt disgust at these monsters and so buried them deep within the earth, in fathomless Tartaros, a gloomy pit as far below the underworld Hades as dark Hades is below the shining heavens.

Gaia grew angry at Ouranos' treatment of their children, and she plotted revenge.

She went to Tartaros and asked, offering a long-bladed sickle, "Which of you, my children, will avenge me on heartless Ouranos?" Only her youngest son, Kronos, accepted the task. The others were frightened.

Handing Kronos the sickle, she warned him, "You must wait until your father is asleep." That night, Kronos sneaked up on Ouranos and cut him with the sickle, dreadfully wounding him. Kronos then forced his bleeding father into fathomless Tartaros. As Ouranos was transported through the air, some of his blood mingled with the ocean foam; from this immortal mixture of Ouranos and ocean, Aphrodite, the goddess of love, was born.

Now Kronos was master of the Titans, and he married the Titaness Rhea. Gaia warned her son, "Just as you were greater than your father, beware or one of your sons shall be greater than you." To prevent this, Kronos imprisoned the immortal babies Rhea had borne him by swallowing them up. The last of these children was shining Zeus. Rhea, instead of allowing Kronos to have baby Zeus as well, fed her husband a stone wrapped in a blanket. Brutal Kronos did not notice the difference but patted his stomach and smiled.

After Zeus had safely grown up in a distant cave, far out of sight of his father, he asked the wise, ever-changing sea nymph Metis to concoct a potion. "This potion," said Zeus to Metis, "must cause my wicked father to cough up my brothers and sisters. I need my siblings to help me, and they cannot do that inside Kronos' belly."

Metis brewed a stomach-turning drink for Kronos and brought it to the terrible Titan.

Kronos sipped and liked the taste. He gulped down the rest, and a moment later out of his big mouth erupted his children—Hades, Poseidon, Demeter, Hera and Hestia.

"I've been tricked!" cried Kronos. "Now my children are loose!"

Indeed they were, delighted to be once again in the fresh air. They thanked Zeus for their rescue and he quickly organized them against their father.

"To arms!" Zeus declared. "Now that we're free, we must defeat him." The gods uprooted mountains and flung them at their father.

Hard-hearted Kronos and many mighty Titans hurled mountains in return; the warfare sounded like thunder on top of thunder. Zeus used the aegis, his tremendous shield, to defend himself from his father's attacks and blasted Kronos and the Titans with terrible lightning bolts that the hard-working Cyclopes forged for him. With Kronos and the Titans dizzy and flat on their backs, Zeus and his siblings imprisoned their foes under mountain ranges or in the pits of Tartaros. The crushed and defeated Titans kicked and stormed, hot with anger, exploding the tops off the mountains that pressed them down. We see even today the fiery volcanos that spew the Titans' fury. Their strong legs still push against the earth's crust, causing earthquakes, but they cannot get out again. With the war's end, Zeus and his brothers divided up their new possessions. This was how Zeus became the god of heaven and ruler of all the gods, and how Poseidon became god of the sea and Hades the god of the underworld.

It was during the peace following the clash of the gods and Titans that wise Metis became pregnant by Zeus. However, Gaia, Mother Earth, warned Zeus that if Metis had a son, he would be greater than Zeus himself. Taking an example from the defeat of cruel

Zeus used the aegis, his tremendous shield, to defend himself from his father's attacks.

Kronos, Zeus swallowed up Metis. Many months later, he had a terrible headache. He went among his friends and begged them to split his head open and allow the pain to get out. None of the gods or Titans dared do such a thing—none but Prometheus, the far-thinking Titan. So far-thinking was he that he had sided with Zeus in the recent war with Kronos, and was thus rewarded with a place among the gods.

"The pain will be sharp," said Prometheus, "but then you'll feel better.—Now put your hands over your eyes." Zeus did so. Down came Prometheus' axe, and crack went Zeus's skull!

Out of his forehead leapt Zeus's brilliant new daughter, Athena, the goddess of wisdom, dressed in a warrior's glimmering armor.

Prometheus quickly patched up with clay the split in Zeus's head, while Zeus roared with laughter. What an entrance for a child! Full-grown and only seconds old.

"Father, dear," she said, "I have many things in mind."

"Indeed you have, as I shared all my thoughts with you before you were born," said Zeus.

Soon after this, Zeus married Hera, his sister. He loved many other immortal and mortal women as well, and had many important children by them. These offspring included the Muses, the Seasons, the Fates, the Graces, the maiden Persephone, Apollo, Artemis, Ares, Hermes and, of course, the great and mighty Hercules.

The Story of Prometheus

Though the gods Zeus, Hades and Poseidon shared power on earth, they were not interested in the clay-like creatures known as mankind. Men did not know how to plow the ground to grow their food; they did not know about weapons, with which they would have been able to hunt animals; they did not know how to speak.

It was Prometheus who first took an interest in mankind; he taught them many skills. The greatest skill, perhaps, was speech. Whatever one man knew, he now could teach another. And soon every man knew how to speak, how to farm, how to hunt and how to use as clothing the skins of the animals they killed. One thing Prometheus was not allowed to teach them was how to cook their food, heat their dwellings or fashion metal weapons. Zeus had ruled that men were not to have the use of godly fire.

Prometheus, not letting himself foresee the punishment Zeus would soon give him, decided to steal fire for mankind. On the slopes of Mount Olympos, Prometheus found a long, flute-stemmed plant, a fennel, and he took it and went to the ever-burning Olympian flame. He reached down and picked up from its base an ash-colored coal and shoved it down into the core of the fennel. With the coal hidden yet burning hot, he casually passed through the court of

Mount Olympos, and waved hello to Zeus. The lord of gods, seeing his friend Prometheus, nodded, smiling, and suspected nothing.

It was later that evening, however, that Zeus, seated upon his glorious throne, was gazing at the first star of the evening. He breathed deeply and his thoughts were filled with pleasure. His mind ranged from the beauties of the colossal universe to the beauties of his wife and daughters. And then, sniffing deeply, he realized that he was smelling smoke—apparently roasted meat—drifting up to the heavens from earth.

Angrily Zeus leaped off his throne and flew down to earth like an arrow. There he saw several men, sitting in a circle around a glowing fire, roasting a fine side of cattle. Zeus thundered, he tossed lightning bolts across the sky, he emptied the heavens of water. The men, however, much to his surprise, covered themselves and their fire with a huge tent of dried animal skins. Zeus was amazed and impressed. These puny men were, after all, rather clever. But who had taught them such skills? Who had given them the immortal gift of fire?

Zeus found Prometheus on the far side of the world. The Titan was talking with his brother, Epimetheus, whose name means "afterthought." Epimetheus thought just as hard and long as Prometheus, only he thought about what he had done rather than what he next meant to do. As a result, he often made mistakes.

Zeus overheard some of their conversation.

"Should the gods offer you a gift, Epimetheus, do

not accept it," Prometheus was saying. "You cannot trust them."

"I trust everyone," said Epimetheus.

"You must not," said his brother, who practiced thinking ahead. "I have a feeling I will not always be around to give you counsel. Please take care."

"If you say so," said Epimetheus.

And now Zeus made himself apparent to the Titans.

"You'll violate the immortal laws, will you?" thundered Zeus, seizing Prometheus. He hurled mankind's first friend through the sky, and Prometheus fell tumbling to earth in the Caucasus mountains. Zeus then ordered the fire god Hephaestus to have Prometheus bound with bronze chains to a cliffside.

Zeus came and saw this deed fulfilled. He declared to Prometheus, "You will be sorry for what you have done."

"I am proud," declared Prometheus. "With fire men can change their world. In the ages before I helped them, they were ignorant; now they are a community of artists and workers."

"With your pride," said Zeus, frowning, "will come suffering!"

Out of the sky came screeching a frightening eagle. It came and grasped poor Prometheus with its claws and then tore its beak through his side. Prometheus screamed.

"Every day," pronounced Zeus, "this eagle will eat away your liver. And every night your liver shall grow back for the eagle's next meal. You will suffer everlasting torment."

Zeus then went and offered to Epimetheus a beautifully crafted creature, who spoke lightly and sweetly, and who walked prettily. By Zeus's order, the immortal craftsman Hephaestus had fashioned the first woman. Her name was Pandora, a Greek word meaning "all gifts." She was Zeus's gift to men. Epimetheus, not paying any mind to the advice of his brother that he not take a god's gift, gladly accepted beautiful Pandora. With Pandora's wardrobe came a sealed wooden box, a box about which Zeus had told the new bride and groom, "This gift is not to be opened."

Pandora was naturally curious. She and Epimetheus were happy, never thinking of tomorrow, delighting in each day. But she couldn't stop wondering about the gift she could not open. "I'll just take a peek," she said to herself one day. "Just a peek, and then I'll close it up again."

Pandora lifted the box and shook it. She heard nothing rattle, and she was puzzled, wondering about the contents. She slipped her finger under the lid of the box and tried to feel around within the box. There were many things! But what, she couldn't tell.

Now she absolutely had to look. She opened the box, and out, like a swarm of insects, flew all the troubles of mankind: Disease, Hunger, Pain. She slammed shut the lid, and one tiny little insect-like creature fell back into the box: Hope! Mankind, which before had known nothing of its own misery, now had full knowledge of it. With Hope, however, mankind can continue to think that better times will come, that suffering will end.

Some say that Zeus's spiteful plan to afflict mankind, in giving it women and knowledge of its suffering, was a generous gift.

The Story of Persephone

Meanwhile, living in the underworld, was Zeus's gloomy brother Hades. Hades was different from his brothers and preferred the company of spirits to the company of the gods on Mount Olympos. He rarely went anywhere.

But one day, wanting to take a look at a summer day, he passed over the earth and saw lovely Persephone, the daughter of the goddess of fertility Demeter and Hades' own brother Zeus. If there was anything lacking in his underworld, it was the presence of a bright, shining bride. Neither god nor man escapes Aphrodite, the goddess of love, and she clouded Hades' mind with desire. Stern, heavy-browed Hades could not think of anything but Persephone. Though immortal, he thought he would die if he did not wed her.

"Brother Zeus," said Hades, having made a trip to Mount Olympos for just this purpose, "I want to marry Persephone, your daughter."

Zeus scratched his forehead, nodding. "I worry that Demeter, the girl's mother, might object. But, after all, you are my brother, and it is high time you took a bride."

The next day, while Persephone was gathering fresh, glorious flowers, Hades appeared out of a hole in the earth and stole her away, carrying her back down to his shadowy kingdom in a winged chariot.

Demeter searched and searched for her daughter, but it was many days before she was able to discover what had happened to Persephone. When she did find out, she ran away from Olympos and refused to speak to the other gods, who had countenanced this outrage. Demeter was deeply saddened by her daughter's marriage and lost her interest in helping the food grow on earth. The grain withered and died, and so did the fruit and vegetables. The mortals prayed to the gods for a return of their crops.

Zeus listened to these prayers, but there was nothing he could do about them without Demeter's consent.

"Please, my darling," said Zeus to Demeter, "return to Olympos and oversee again the earthly harvests for mankind."

"Never," said Demeter. "Not until I see my daughter."

Zeus had no choice but to send for Persephone. Hades, receiving his brother's message from Hermes, said he would allow his bride to visit Mount Olympos. "But before you go," said Hades to Persephone, who was eager to leave, "have something to eat to tide you over: it's a long trip." And she took from him a few seeds of sweet pomegranate and then flew away with Hermes to Olympos.

Seeing her mother, Persephone rushed into her arms and wept. Zeus nodded and smiled.

"My daughter," Demeter asked Persephone, "are you unhappy in Hades?"

"It is dark," she answered. "And it is lonely."

"Would you rather return to the grain-covered earth?" asked Demeter. "And to me, your mother?"

"Indeed I would," said pale Persephone.

"But tell me this," said Zeus, "have you eaten anything while you were down there?"

"No," said Persephone. "Well, almost nothing! Just three pomegranate seeds!"

Zeus and Demeter shook their heads. Anyone who eats while in the underworld can never again return full-time to the earth or Mount Olympos. Persephone had not known this, and so now she wept again.

"But for two-thirds of the year," said father Zeus, "you may live with your mother on earth."

Demeter and Persephone realized that this compromise was the best they could now hope for and accepted Zeus's ruling.

Even Hades thought this arrangement would be for the best. Living in the underworld is not easy for anybody. That it happened to suit Hades was his good fortune. He understood that Persephone would probably be happier while with him if she knew she would shortly be returning for her seasons with Demeter.

Chapter II
Hercules

HERCULES, THE son of almighty Zeus and beautiful mortal Alcmene, was the strongest man who ever lived. Now when Hercules was eight months old, he woke one night to find a monstrous snake had coiled itself around him. Instead of crying out, baby Hercules wrapped his tiny powerful hands around the meaty throat of the snake and choked it to death.

As a boy he had many wise teachers, including the centaur Cheiron, and he was soon a master of wrestling and archery. He was handsome and had blazing eyes. There was nothing Hercules feared.

When he was eighteen years old, he went out to kill a raging lion that had been destroying the farmers' cattle. He smashed its head with his club, killing it, and took off its skin. He wore its fur over his shoulders, with the lion's head as his cap.

Hercules was so bold and so great that the gods, especially his father Zeus, wanted him to be one of themselves—an immortal.

The only immortal against this was Hera, Zeus's wife.

"A god!" she said with outrage. "He? The son of a

13

ridiculous woman! If you insist on his becoming a god, he must do a god's work!"

And so began a nearly impossible series of ten chores, the Labors of Hercules.

"If, and only if, you complete the labors King Eurystheus gives you," said Hera, "then you may live among us on Mount Olympos."

Eurystheus of Tiryns did not like this strong young man, and for the first task gave Hercules one he thought would be fatal. "Kill the Nemean lion," he ordered.

This lion was much more terrible than the previous beast Hercules had killed. Hercules shot arrow after arrow at it, which only made the Nemean lion yawn, for the arrows could not pierce its skin. Hercules then went after it with his bare hands. The savage Nemean lion roared, and it slashed at Hercules with its claws. Hercules wrestled it, threw it on the ground and then choked it by its shaggy neck until it died.

When Hercules returned to Tiryns, the king was so frightened by Hercules' success that he did not allow the man to come into his palace. Eurystheus called to him from a high window and assigned him his second labor, another task he was sure would kill mighty Hercules: "Go and destroy the Hydra in Lerna."

This Hydra was a snaky creature that had nine heads, the one in the middle being immortal. It lived in a cave, from which it would come out in order to feast on cattle. When Hercules came to Lerna, it was asleep in its cave. Hercules listened. All he heard was a snaky whistling: "Whewsh! Whewsh!" Hercules shot fire-tipped arrows into the cave until the Hydra, angered by this nuisance, sprang out at him. Hercules leaped upon the fierce Hydra's neck, swinging his sword and chopping off its heads. But for every head he cut off, two more grew back. Within minutes there were hundreds of Hydra heads hissing at him and longing to devour him. Hercules called to his friend Iolaus, who had made the journey with him, to bring a torch. This time as Hercules cut off the newly sprung heads, he and his friend burned and sealed the necks before the heads could grow back. This worked well; and, even though a crab, friendly to the Hydra, tried to annoy him, pinching his toes and ankles, Hercules finally chopped off the unkillable last head. He buried it under a tremendous rock, where it still lives, hissing but unable to move. The Hydra's snaky body Hercules cut up, squeezing out its poison to use on his arrows.

When he returned to the king and told him of his success, the king, a cheating sort of man, said, "No, you get no credit for that labor. You had help from your friend. What I want now is the sacred Ceryntian deer!"

This deer had golden antlers, and it belonged to the goddess of hunting, Artemis. Hercules dared not kill a goddess's deer, and so for one entire year he tracked it, finally wearing it out with the chase. He now captured it alive. Artemis forgave Hercules, as he had not hurt her beautiful deer, and she allowed him to bring it to the king.

"Very clever," remarked Eurystheus, stroking the

As Hercules cut off the newly sprung heads, he and his friend burned and sealed the necks.

golden antlers. "But you'll have to have an even better plan now. Your next labor is to bring me the Erymanthian boar alive."

A wild, fierce boar is not easy to kill, but it is easier to kill one than to catch it alive. This, however, was what Hercules succeeded in doing. He chased it into the deepest fields of newly fallen snow. Its head could barely rise above the snow banks. Each new turn it took sank it in powdery fluff. It became so tired, it only snorted with relief when Hercules picked it up and threw it over his mighty shoulders.

After he brought the boar to Eurystheus, Hercules set out for a short while with Jason and the Argonauts, who were leaving on their great sailing adventure in quest of the Golden Fleece. The Argonauts honored him as a hero, but when he was late for their departure from an island, they left him behind. He had been searching for his missing friend Hylas. Hercules eventually made his way back to Tiryns and asked Eurystheus for his next labor.

This labor was the dirtiest ever performed. "Your fifth labor," said Eurystheus, "is to clean out the Augean stables in one single day." Augeas was a neighboring king, and he had herds and herds of cattle. The stables were filled with cow dung, as Augeas, a king with too much pride, would never bother to clean them out.

Hercules proceeded to the land of Augeas, where, holding his nose, he offered the king his services.

"I'd like to clean out your stables today," said Hercules.

"Help yourself," said Augeas. "I don't want to do it. I'll pay you a good sum of gold should you succeed."

Before the day was out, the mighty son of Zeus had diverted the paths of two rivers through the stables, and so washed all the filth away.

"I am not going to count that labor," said King Eurystheus, "for I have learned that you were paid for it. For your next task, go chase away the nasty Stymphalian birds."

Hercules went off to Lake Stymphalos, and was amazed by the number of birds. There were too many for him to kill, and he wondered if he would fail in this labor. But good, wise Athena came to him from Mount Olympos and gave him a pair of brass castanets. Hercules stood upon a mountain overlooking the lake and knocked these castanets together. The birds screeched and cawed, flying away from the horrible din Hercules was creating.

Once they were all gone, Hercules returned to Tiryns.

"What cannot you do?" said Eurystheus.

"I do not know," replied Hercules.

"Then kindly bring me the savage Cretan bull, that father of the Minotaur—but do not kill it."

"As you wish," said Hercules. He went across the sea to Crete and, as usual, captured the requested animal. When he returned with it to Tiryns, the king was amazed.

Hercules then released the bull. The bull bucked and stormed, and ran crazily through the countryside.

"The next labor, Hercules," said the king, "is to bring me the man-eating horses of Diomedes." These four beasts were so fierce they ate men as hungrily as other horses eat apples.

But before he came to these horses in Thrace, he stopped in Pherae and performed one of his greatest feats—he wrestled Death itself for the life of Alcestis. She was the wife of Hercules' friend Admetus, and she had offered herself to Death in the place of her husband. When Hercules arrived at Admetus' palace, he found everyone in gloom, grieving for Alcestis. As a gift to his friend, Hercules went to the tomb of Alcestis. He found Death drinking the funeral offerings her family had left there. Hercules grabbed Death from behind, pinning his arms.

"Give me back Alcestis, and I shall free you," declared Hercules.

Death struggled, groaning, but could not free himself from the muscular arms of the son of Zeus. "Very well," cried Death, "you have won. Take her back to Admetus. But some day I shall return for her—and for you!"

"Indeed," answered Hercules, "but not for many years—when Alcestis is old and gray. As for me, I will gain immortality and avoid your cold grip."

Admetus was overjoyed by Hercules' rescue of his wife and asked Hercules to stay on as his guest. But Hercules had more labors to accomplish.

From Pherae, Hercules went off to Thrace to find Diomedes' fierce horses. He tamed them and rounded them up, bringing them down to the sea, and soon after delivered them to Eurystheus.

The ninth labor seemed more difficult.

"I want the Amazon Hippolyte's belt," said Eurystheus. Queen Hippolyte had received this belt from the war god Ares, because she was the greatest warrior in that battle-loving nation of women. Hercules came to her in a humble fashion, simply telling her who he was and what he needed. Hippolyte was so pleased to meet the famous Hercules that she agreed to give him her belt. As she unfastened it, her women warriors, jealous of their queen's kind looks on Hercules, attacked the hero. In the battle, all was confusion, and unhappy Hercules accidentally killed poor Hippolyte. He sorrowfully took the belt and returned with it to Tiryns.

"Bring me the cattle of Geryon," said King Eurystheus.

Hercules set out and on the island of Erythia met the monstrous cowherd Geryon, a three-bodied man, joined together at the waist. His watchdog was the two-headed Orthos. The double-barking canine attacked Hercules, but the son of Zeus clubbed its brains from its heads. Then Geryon, all three of him, rushed at Hercules. Mighty Hercules did not know which part of Geryon to kill first. He stepped back and shot an arrow at Geryon's middle, killing him altogether. Hercules then captured Geryon's cattle.

Hercules had performed ten labors, but Eurystheus was not willing to count Hercules' destruction of the

Hydra, since he had had help, or the cleaning of the Augean stables, for which he had been paid. Eurystheus insisted on two more labors, and Hercules agreed to do them. The eleventh labor was to go and get the splendid golden apples of the Hesperides, near where mighty Atlas held up the sky.

Before Hercules reached Atlas, he rescued Atlas' brother, Prometheus, whom Zeus had bound to a cliff to be pecked at every day by a bloodthirsty eagle. Hercules slew the eagle and cut off Zeus's bands. Prometheus, in thanks, told Hercules not to try to get the golden apples himself, but to ask Atlas to do it for him.

The great Titan Atlas, standing at the edge of the world, had been straining under the weight of the sky, keeping it from crushing the earth, ever since Zeus assigned him this task. This was Atlas' punishment for having fought against Zeus in the fateful war with Kronos.

Mighty Hercules came and asked Atlas if he knew where the golden apples were.

Atlas said, "Yes, I do. They're just over there in my garden. Help yourself." But there was a huge and hungry snake the size of a dragon guarding the apple tree.

Hercules replied, "Perhaps you would like a rest from your duty? I could hold up the sky for you while you went in and picked me a few apples."

Atlas thought about this for a moment, and then agreed.

When he returned with the apples—the snake had not dared to bother him—and saw Hercules stooping and straining beneath the sky's weight, he realized how glad he was to have been relieved of that tedious task.

He saw this as a chance to pass off his duty onto Hercules. "My friend," he said, "you are doing such a good job in my stead, I will let you go on doing it."

Hercules understood Atlas' trick. "Very well, mighty Titan. It's no trouble to me. But wait a moment. Before you go, would you mind holding the sky while I put a soft pad across my head and shoulders?"

Atlas, though the brother of clever Prometheus, wasn't so smart. He set down the apples he had fetched for Hercules and laughed, saying, "I myself have never needed a cushion. But, all right, let me lend you a hand."

As Hercules stepped out from underneath the sky, Atlas shouldered the burden. He watched Hercules pick up the apples.

"But you're staying here!" cried Atlas. "You won't need those!"

"Farewell, Atlas!" said Hercules, going on his way.

Atlas stamped his foot, but he couldn't do anything about Hercules' deceitful trick.

The final labor that Eurystheus gave Hercules was to fetch the terrible watchdog of Hades, three-headed Cerberus. Hercules journeyed into the underworld and asked Hades himself for permission to borrow his dog. Hades answered, "Go right ahead, nephew,

by all means. But use no weapon to make him follow
you."

Hercules pulled his lion skin tight over his body
and crept up on the keen-eyed dog. Just as the dog's
heads began to bark, Hercules sprang and wrestled
the beast until it gave up the fight and rolled over
and, showing its belly, licked Hercules' hands. It
followed him away from the gloomy underworld to
King Eurystheus. The king shuddered at the sight of
the dog he would see all too soon.

"Take him away!" cried Eurystheus. "And leave me
alone. You have performed your labors. Now go!"

Hercules laughed at the cowardly king and led the
bewildered dog back home.

The mighty son of Zeus had succeeded in his
labors, earning the right to live forever among the
Olympian gods.

Chapter III

Heroes and Monsters

Perseus and Medusa

F OUL MEDUSA! Instead of hair, she had hissing poisonous snakes. Her face was somewhat green, somewhat blue, and her eyes an awful shade of red. To look at her would turn any mortal man or woman to stone. And so Medusa had no friends to speak to or to love, just her immortal sisters, the dreadful Gorgons.

A king named Polydectes longed to marry Perseus' mother, Danae, but to win her he needed to get Perseus out of the way. He asked Perseus to do such a dangerous deed that he would be killed in attempting it. "Fetch me the head of Medusa," said Polydectes.

Perseus could not do such a thing alone, and prayed for help from the gods, especially the wise Athena.

Athena appeared to him and said, "You need several things if you mean to get close to the Gorgons. Use this bright shield, my shining aegis, as a mirror when you approach the Gorgons. Do not look directly at them. And use this sickle of Hermes to cut off Medusa's head. You need to be able to fly, so that after you cut off Medusa's head her winged sisters cannot chase you down; in addition, you had better be invisible, or they might not give up the chase. To gain the gifts of flight and invisibility you must find the nymphs who live in the River Styx, the dark waters of Hades. I may not reveal to you the way to the Styx, and the only beings that may are the Graiai. At the ends of the earth, in a cave, live the three sisters, so old they have but a single eye left among them, which they share by passing it back and forth, and one tooth, which they also share. You must convince them to tell you where to go."

Perseus thanked Athena and set out over the seas and across the desert until he reached the Graiai.

"What do you want?" said one Graia.

"Directions to the Styx," said Perseus.

"Ah, yes, wouldn't you like to know," said another Graia.

"Ah, yes, wouldn't he like to know," said the third.

They laughed at this traveler who dared ask them for help, and they passed their eye back and forth to take a mocking look at him.

As the last Graia was returning it to the first, Perseus, angry at their laughter, quickly stepped forward and snatched the eyeball.

"What's he doing now?" asked the Graiai among themselves.

"I can't see!" said the first Graia. "Give me the eye."

"I don't have it," said the other two.

"I have it," said Perseus, "and I will not return it until you tell me how to get to the River Styx."

The Graiai grumbled, but what was there to do? They valued the little bit of sight they had left, and so they told him. The hero went off and after many days reached the nymphs in the Styx.

"How did you ever find us, handsome one?" asked a nymph.

"It was not easy," he replied. "But now that I am here, will you help me?"

"We'd be happy to do so," said the nymphs. They strapped onto his feet the sandals of Hades that enabled him to fly. They handed him a large bag into which he could put Medusa's ugly head. Then they kissed him and set a cap on his head that made him invisible. They wished him luck, and Perseus thanked them and flew off.

Once he got into the neighborhood of the Gorgons he saw dozens of statues sculpted in horrified poses. They were men who had turned to stone after glancing at Medusa or her sisters. Perseus, however, was invisible and so the Gorgons did not notice him as he approached. They liked jumping out at foolish men and yapping, "Look at me!"

As he got closer Perseus turned about and lifted up his shield to use as a mirror. That way he could watch them and see where he was going. When he caught a glimpse of their distorted reflection, he found it so hideous that he decided to wait until it was dark to attack.

Finally night covered the land with darkness, and Perseus crept closer and closer to the sisters. He saw that even their snaky hair had fallen peacefully asleep upon the smooth stones they used for pillows.

Perseus now flew forward, and in a large sweeping motion sliced off Medusa's slimy head. He jumped back then, as out of her neck sprang a horse, Pegasus, who neighed loudly and flapped its beautiful wings. Immortal Pegasus flew off to Mount Olympos, where he became a favorite of the gods.

Perseus now flew home. In the palace he found that King Polydectes had married Perseus' mother, Danae, against her will.

Polydectes was unhappy to see Perseus again. "I don't suppose you have really fetched me what I asked for," the king said. "Therefore, you must leave our country and never come back."

"But I have done what you asked," said Perseus. "Just take a look and see for yourself."

He tossed the king the bag, and then went to his mother and covered her eyes and his own with Athena's shield. The king, on the other hand, and all his men gazed with wonder at the bag and then the king opened it and brought forth Medusa's ghastly head. All of them who looked gaped in amazement, and all were turned to stone.

Perseus shielded his eyes and went and replaced Medusa's head in the bag. He called on the goddess

Athena, and when she appeared he thanked her, returned to her her shield and presented her with the bag as a gift. The gods can tolerate amazing ugliness, and so she gladly accepted Medusa's head. In fact, the image of Medusa's face was forever after etched onto Athena's wondrous aegis.

Bellerophon and Pegasus

When brave young Bellerophon came to Lycia, the king Iobates found him charming. The king had never met a visitor he liked so well. Only after several days did Iobates ask Bellerophon what had brought him to this country.

"The king of Ephyra sent me to deliver this note," replied Bellerophon.

The king of Ephyra was the husband of Iobates' daughter. Iobates read the message: "This man has offended me and your daughter. I request you to give him a task that will bring on his death."

Iobates was surprised by this request but did not think of disregarding it. He did not know that Bellerophon had been wrongly accused; he therefore asked him to destroy the Chimera, a creature part lion, part goat and part snake who breathed fire and was then destroying the countryside in Lycia.

The gods had a fondness for handsome Bellerophon, and when he went to Athena's temple to ask for help in this challenge, Sleep filled his body, and Athena, the goddess of wisdom, spoke to him in a dream. "Take this bridle," she said, handing him a lovely golden rope, "and catch Pegasus, the divine winged horse. Riding Pegasus, you will have a chance to destroy the horrible one."

When Bellerophon woke from his dream, there was indeed a golden bridle in his fist, and he set out to find Pegasus, who, you remember, leapt out of Medusa's body when Perseus cut off her ugly head. In a pasture near Mount Olympos, Bellerophon found Pegasus. The horse, seeing Athena's bridle, did not run or fly from the warrior. Bellerophon got up on Pegasus, and the horse, understanding its mission, flew towards Lycia.

The Chimera saw her flying enemy and coughed fiery blasts at what it thought was food. But what kind of food was this? A creature atop the flying horse shot arrow after arrow at her. The Chimera was furious, and Bellerophon, had not Pegasus been so brave, would have turned away in caution.

Pegasus flew them close by the Chimera, around and around her terrible head, confusing her until she got dizzy and fell over in a tumble. And now Bellerophon saw his chance. Tipping his arrows with bronze, he fired them down into the beast's ghastly mouth. The Chimera began to choke; its fiery breath melted the bronze, which flowed down her tender throat and into her stomach. She leapt to her feet, in horrible pain, and nearly thrashed Pegasus and Bellerophon out of the sky. But it was too late for the

Chimera. Her tender insides were a volcano of liquid metal. She coughed up one last blast of fire and perished in a heap of ashes.

Bellerophon had won. Pegasus brought him back to a surprised King Iobates and then flew off to Zeus on Mount Olympos.

Theseus and the Minotaur

On the island of Crete lived King Minos. He had many children by his wife, Pasiphae. When Minos forgot to pay his respects to Poseidon, the god of the sea, Poseidon punished him. The sea god asked for the love goddess Aphrodite's help to make Pasiphae fall in love with a bull. By this animal, then, Pasiphae had a strange child, a bull-headed monster called the Minotaur.

Minos was so ashamed of this beast that he asked the great inventor Daedalus to construct a pen from which the Minotaur could not escape. Daedalus built a vast maze, a labyrinth, from which no man could ever get out once he entered.

The Minotaur lived within this labyrinth roaring with anger. To quiet him, Minos sent prisoners from Athens into the labyrinth. The Minotaur hunted these men down and killed them, and this was his only occupation.

A young man named Theseus, the son of Athens' king, sailed to Crete to try to stop these sacrifices of

Athenians. His father Aegeus begged him not to go, but Theseus insisted. So his father told him that if his mission to Minos was successful to take down the ship's black sail on the return voyage and raise the white one. "Then I will know and not have to wonder whether you are still alive," said Aegeus.

When Theseus arrived in Crete he went to Minos and said, "Athens has paid you tribute long enough."

Minos laughed at him and said, "I defeated your country in the war, and I may do whatever I like with my prisoners. If you don't like what the Minotaur does, go and kill him, and I will demand no more Athenians."

"That is what I shall do," replied Theseus.

Ariadne, a young and beautiful daughter of Minos, saw Theseus and fell in love with him. She could not bear the thought that he would enter the labyrinth and never return. She went and begged the inventor of the labyrinth, Daedalus, for the secret to get back out safely from the maze. Ariadne was so sweet that Daedalus told her what to do.

She secretly went to Theseus and said, "Take this ball of thread and tie it to the gateway of the labyrinth. Hold onto the ball and unwind the thread as you make your way in. Once you kill the Minotaur—for I see that you have the strength and courage to do so—you will be able to find your way back by following the thread."

And so Theseus unwound the thread on the way in, and found the man-eating Minotaur. Theseus had no weapons, but his fists were like bronze. When the Minotaur tried to swallow him up, he gripped one arm around its neck and battered the creature with the other. The Minotaur fell over dead!

Theseus followed the string back out of the winding labyrinth. But when he presented himself to Minos, the king was furious. "You have killed my beast! You have solved the riddle of the labyrinth! For these deeds, I shall have you killed!"

Theseus, however, battled off Minos' soldiers, and made his way down to his ship. Minos' daughter Ariadne rushed down to the shore and begged that Theseus take her with him. He agreed and they escaped and sailed away.

Lovely Ariadne, who had betrayed her father because of her love for Theseus, died before the ship arrived in Athens. This so saddened Theseus that he forgot to raise his white sail that would have signaled to Aegeus his successful adventure. Theseus' poor father, seeing the black sail and feeling he had nothing and no one left to live for, jumped off a cliff to his death.

Theseus became king of Athens and never allowed his citizens to be sent to the labyrinth in Crete again.

Daedalus and Icarus

Meanwhile, for having helped Theseus, Minos imprisoned both Daedalus and Daedalus' son, Icarus, in the labyrinth.

"Will we die, father?" asked Icarus.

"We all die some time," said Daedalus. "But if I can finish these wings, our time will not be as soon. We're going to fly away from here."

Daedalus built two pairs of wings for himself and Icarus. Each was made of feathers and wax on a wooden frame. Inventors often know the flaws of their inventions. The flaw in these wings was that if they got too close to the sea, the salt spray would dampen the wings—making them too heavy to fly. "So don't get them wet!" said Daedalus to his son.

"I won't!"

"On the other hand, if the wings get too hot," continued Daedalus, "the wax will melt and the wings will come apart. Do you understand? Don't fly too low, don't fly too high."

Icarus, impatient to get up in the air, said, "I know! I know!" His father's advice was already forgotten.

They set out, the people of Crete marvelling at the men as they rose from the labyrinth like birds and flew away over the ocean. Daedalus called out, "Follow me, Icarus!"

Icarus shouted back, "I'll be right there, Father." Icarus soared, he flew higher and higher—he felt like a god! Daedalus hovered in the middle sky, pleading with his son to show some sense. But, just as Daedalus feared, the wax melted off Icarus' wings; they were in tatters and the feathers were slipping away.

"Father!" screamed Icarus. He was now plunging toward the sea. What could Daedalus do? He flew around and around, over the very spot where the waters had swallowed up his son. Daedalus, after weeping tears on Icarus' watery grave, winged his way to distant Sicily. It was Icarus' fatal fall that gave these waters their name, the Icarian Sea.

The Story of Narcissus

One fine day the youth Narcissus was walking on a path along a forest stream when he came to a smooth, clear, deep running pool. He was thirsty, and so he went to the bank of the stream and knelt down and leaned over the water. Who do you think he saw down there looking up at him? He did not know, but whoever it was was the most fascinating and handsome young man he had ever seen.

Narcissus smiled, and the handsome young man smiled at the same time. How charming! He felt there was some secret connection between himself and the young man, and that they needed no words to understand each other.

He and his admirer, who dwelled below the surface of the pond, stared at each other all day. When night came, Narcissus' admirer seemed to swim away into the darkness. Narcissus got up and went on his way, terribly in love.

The moon came out and the lonely nymph named Echo heard the words of this handsome young man.

"I am in love," said Narcissus. "What a handsome young man!"

"I am in love," said Echo. "What a handsome young man!" It was true, Narcissus was remarkably handsome. Echo now appeared to Narcissus, her arms open in love, but he turned away, not wanting to see anyone, not even a beautiful immortal nymph, if she did not resemble the lovely young man he had seen.

Echo followed Narcissus everywhere, unable to say anything original, always only saying what he had said. He did not enjoy this. He only had thoughts for one person.

Each day he returned to the pool in the forest, and each day he and his admirer gazed in wonder, silently, lovingly. Each night Echo followed him home repeating everything he said, trying to please him with her agreement.

And then one day, Narcissus, tired of the distance between himself and his true love, looked into his eyes and their eyes agreed: Narcissus should join his loved one. In the pool? Yes. Narcissus could not swim, but his admirer, this one who seemed to understand Narcissus' own soul, encouraged him. Narcissus reached out his arms to the young man and the young man reached out his arms as well. Into the pool plunged Narcissus!

Echo rushed to the pond and looked in. There she saw only her own reflection. Narcissus had sunk to the bottom of the pool and drowned in his love for himself. In his memory we now find lovely blooming narcissus flowers growing by still pools.

Echo wept. She was now so lonely and heartbroken

that she wasted away, until all that remained of her was a voice, speechless unless spoken to.

Oedipus

When Oedipus was born to the king and queen of Thebes, Laius and Iocasta, a prophet announced that the baby would grow up to kill his father and marry his mother. To avoid such a shocking outcome, King Laius sorrowfully ordered one of his servants to kill the baby.

The servant took the baby away, onto a hilltop, but he could not kill the innocent child. He left Oedipus instead with a shepherd, who brought him across the mountains to the king of Corinth. This king claimed the boy and raised him as his own.

When Oedipus grew to manhood, a prophet warned him that he would kill his father and marry his mother. Not knowing that he had been adopted, and that his real parents were Iocasta and Laius, Oedipus left the country to avoid committing such crimes. While crossing over the mountain, he fought a caravan of men who tried to force him off the road. He killed them all.

From there, Oedipus came to the outskirts of Thebes, which he did not know was his original country. Thebes was being menaced then by the Sphinx, who would ask its visitors a riddle. When they could not answer correctly, the Sphinx would kill them. The riddle was this: "What has four legs, two legs, and then three legs?" Oedipus was good at solving riddles and went to the Sphinx, who asked him its question. Oedipus thought for a moment and then answered, "A man! As a baby he crawls on his hands and knees, as an adult he walks on his two legs, as an old man he walks with a cane!" The Sphinx, shocked by this mortal's correct answer, fell over dead. As a reward from the Theban people, Oedipus was named king, for the former king had recently been killed. His bride was the queen, Iocasta.

Several years later, after they had had four children, plagues began to destroy the people of Thebes. Oedipus strove to discover the reason. A prophecy gave him a hint, that the murderer of the former king, Laius, was living unpunished in Thebes. Until this murder was punished, plagues would sweep the country.

Oedipus questioned everyone: old servants, his wife, his brother-in-law, and the famous seer Teiresias. As he questioned them about the former king's death, he slowly put together the facts, the terrible facts that seemed to point to himself!

At last, the entire mystery revealed itself to him. He understood who his true parents were—Iocasta and Laius. One of those men he had killed while crossing over the mountain had been his father! He himself had killed Laius! Cursing his fate that had doomed him to do what he had meant not to do, he blinded himself, as he could not bear to see the children he

Oedipus was good at solving riddles and went to the Sphinx, who asked him its question.

had fathered with Iocasta, his wife and mother. Iocasta for her part hanged herself.

Oedipus, in disgrace, left his country, and, as a blind beggar, wandered the countryside. Oedipus was the unhappiest man who ever was. He lived in suffering to an old age, accompanied by his daughter Antigone, until the gods, pitying his pain, whisked him off the face of the earth at a sacred place near Athens.

Chapter IV
The Argonauts

PELIAS, THE king of Iolcus, lived in dread of a man who would enter his palace wearing one sandal— the other foot bare. This man, a prophet had told Pelias, would bring him death.

One day a handsome young man crossed the Anaurus River to Iolcus, and one of his sandals came off in the mucky river. He then presented himself to the king.

"Who are you?" asked Pelias, noticing the man's bare foot. "Why have you come?"

"I am Jason, son of Iason, the man from whom you stole this kingdom. I have returned to claim our rights."

"I will step down and restore the kingdom to your family," said Pelias, "on one condition. You must bring to me the Golden Fleece."

The Golden Fleece was the woolly coat of the sea god Poseidon's golden ram. It was spread out over the top branches of a sacred oak tree and guarded by an immortal, dragon-sized snake who never slept. To capture such a prize was surely an impossible request, but Jason was young and brave, and replied, "Very well."

Jason asked Argus to build him a ship. The wise goddess Athena advised Argus in the building of this fifty-oared ship called the *Argo*. She even brought him a piece of talking timber to build into the ship—to tell the sailors how to sail it.

Jason rounded up a crew for this adventure, all of them strong men, all of them either sons or grandsons of gods. Jason himself was the grandson of the keeper of the winds, Aiolos. These great men were known as the Argonauts, the sailors of the clever ship *Argo*. One was Peleus, husband of the nereid, or sea-nymph, Thetis and father of Achilles. Another, you might recall, was the invincible Hercules. When they asked him to be their captain, he refused, saying, "The man who gathered us is the man who ought to lead us—Jason."

As they rowed away from Iolcus, their armor glimmering like fire in the bright sun, the people cried and moaned, wondering why Pelias was sending the fine young men to their deaths. Jason's old father, Iason, wept from his sick-bed.

Orpheus, son of the Muse Calliope, sang and played to the men as they rowed. His voice and music were so charming that the men's hearts were light, even when their muscles ached and grew heavy.

Handsome Jason wore a breathtaking cloak, the gift of goddess Athena, and he led the men to an island of widowed women, where they were detained by the widows' wishes. From there they sailed to another island, where Hylas, Hercules' dear friend, was pulled into a deep, dark pool by a lovely nymph. This nymph made Hylas her water-breathing husband, while Hercules wandered the island in despair, looking for his friend. Jason felt he had no choice but to lead his Argonauts back to sea, leaving Hercules behind. In any case, it had become time for Hercules to return to his labors.

They landed next on a beach within a wide bay. There the Argonauts encountered the surly, brutal king Amycus.

He said: "No crew that stops here can pass on until I box one of them. Send out your best man against me and give him your prayers."

The Argonauts were angry at such a greeting, and sent out Polydeuces against him. Amycus was built like a monster; he had a brutal face and massive arms, legs and shoulders. Polydeuces, on the other hand, was strong and quick, like a young tiger. They tied on boxing gloves and began. When Amycus swung his weighty hands at Polydeuces, the younger man turned and took the blow on his shoulder, and then struck the wicked king above his ear. Down fell Amycus, and then Amycus' men sprang at the Argonauts, who cut them down in moments.

The next day they sailed and came to a spot up the coast, where Phineas the prophet, a priest of the god Apollo, lived. Phineas was a tormented old man. When he was a younger man, he had been amazed by his visions of what would be, excited about knowing what only the gods know, and he had told everything! He did not remember that the gods want men to be ignorant of some things. To punish Phineas, Zeus blinded him and ordered the hideous flying Harpies to snatch away any food the once-proud man could beg.

Those men and women who had received the aid of Phineas' prophecies still brought him meals, and yet the Harpies never missed their chance to speed down from the sky and steal the food—even as Phineas raised a piece of it to his mouth. By the time Jason and the Argonauts came to see him, he was old and creaky. He complained to them of the Harpies, and then told them: "I once saw in my future that two sons of the winds would drive these vultures away."

Two of the Argonauts were indeed sons of Boreas, the North Wind. They decided to lure the Harpies down to Phineas so that they could destroy the annoying creatures. A meal was prepared and set before the starving old man. Phineas reached out for the food, and for a moment it seemed that perhaps the Harpies were wary of the sword-bearing Argonauts standing beside the old man. They were nowhere to be seen. But then, as some glorious bread touched Phineas' poor dry lips, the Harpies flashed by like lightning bolts, stealing the bread and all the other food laid out before him.

With another flash they were gone, streaking across the sky. In another moment, the sons of the North Wind, Zetes and Calais, set out in stormy pursuit. And they would have caught the Harpies too, had not Iris, the goddess of the rainbow, called off the chase.

"Sons of the North Wind, halt! The Harpies are Zeus's servants. You may not destroy them. They are useful for reminding men of Zeus's anger. You have done enough. I swear to you that you have now relieved Phineas of his punishment. The Harpies shall return no more to torment him. Go back, and give him this message."

The sons of the North Wind, though hot with the pursuit, relented, and obeyed lovely Iris.

That evening Phineas enjoyed a wondrous meal with the Argonauts and afterwards told them of some of their dangerous adventures to come and how to avoid some of their coming trouble. "But I may not tell you everything," said Phineas, "as the gods will not allow that."

One danger he warned them of was their next, the Clashing Rocks: "No one has ever made it past them! Unlike other rocks, these move from place to place, smashing into each other and sliding apart. Before you try to pass between them, send a dove from your ship, and if it makes it through alive, quickly follow—row hard, row fast."

The Argonauts sailed away from Phineas, thanking him for his advice. After some while, they came to the narrow straits, at the end of which they would find the Clashing Rocks. They heard the thundrous crashing before they saw the rocks, and when they saw them, the water shooting high up between them, they were terrified. They released the dove and watched it fly along the momentary passage between the immense rocks. Just as it passed through, the Clashing Rocks came together with a smash, clipping off the end of the dove's tail feathers. But it had made it through alive, and Jason commanded his men to row like the wind. The rocks were opening out again, and the goddess Athena flew down from Olympos to give the sailors her aid. They had rowed themselves between the two rocks, but before they could get through, the backflow of water into the passage held them there, no matter how hard they rowed. A wave crashed just under them, and the men cried out. The *Argo* could not move!

Athena, unseen by them, now reached out and held the sharp-cliffed rock on their left with one hand and pushed the *Argo* along with her other. She held the rock for only a moment before she let go and the rocks came clashing together, clipping off the tip of their carved stern. The *Argo* had made it!

Athena flew back to Olympos, while the Clashing Rocks, having felt her immortal touch, remained fixed to that spot forever after.

The Argonauts sailed on for weeks, stopping and feasting at numerous islands and coastlands, but avoiding the home of the women warriors, the daughters of Ares known as Amazons. On a distant island they met the shipwrecked sons of Phrixus, who had sailed from Colchis, the very land to which the Argonauts meant to go.

"The gods must have brought you to us," said Jason to Phrixus' sons. "For as you need our help to return to Colchis, we need yours to get there so that we might ask King Aeetes for permission to take the Golden Fleece."

Argus, the first of Phrixus' sons, looked worried at this news. "King Aeetes is not a pleasant man and will not likely give you permission."

But Peleus and the other Argonauts convinced them that Aeetes would be no danger to them, and the sons of Phrixus decided to lead them to Colchis.

Jason was a favorite of Hera and Athena. When they thought of cold-hearted Aeetes, they decided that Jason would never be able to convince the king to allow him to take the Golden Fleece. So they asked the goddess of love, Aphrodite, to convince her naughty child Eros to help their mortal hero. Eros, who shoots the arrows that strike the hearts of lovers, agreed, and sat at Jason's feet as he plucked his bow at Medea, Aeetes' daughter, who was a beautiful young sorceress. Even without the help of Eros' piercing dart, Medea might have fallen in love with Jason, who was very handsome.

When Jason went to Aeetes to ask his consent to row up the river to the grand old oak that held the Golden Fleece, stern Aeetes said, "I grant you, Jason, my consent to fetch the Golden Fleece on one condition: you must do, young man, what I myself do for daily exercise. I yoke my bulls, those two in the pasture there. They snort fire, and their hooves are solid bronze. I then use them to plow a rocky field. And then, instead of planting grain, I plant the teeth of a dragon, which sprout on the spot as fierce, spear-carrying warriors. I kill them all. Can you do this? If not, I must ask you to leave now and never return."

Jason doubted his strength for such a deed, but he agreed to try.

Little did Jason know that Medea was now more faithful to her love for him than to her father. She had a dream, and in it she imagined that the handsome sailor had not come to Colchis for a Golden Fleece but for herself, Medea. She woke and left her palace to find her loved one. Seeing him, her eyes filled with tears, her cheeks turned red, and pain shot through her neck and heart.

"I will help you," said Medea. "In the morning, take this charm, and melt it, and then rub it over your body. It will give you strength. Rub it on your sword and shield and spear. My father's savage bulls will not be able to hurt you. For that one day, you will be invincible. After you yoke the bulls and plow the field and plant the dragon teeth, wait until the warriors rise up from the teeth. Toss a boulder at them, and they will go after the boulder and each other. Kill them off, and then go up the river for the Golden Fleece. It is that simple.—You will remember my help to you, won't you?"

"I will never forget it. And if you come with us, I shall marry you," said Jason.

The next morning, to the amazement of all, Jason, following Medea's directions and using her charm on his body and weapons, yoked the flame-snorting bulls, plowed the hard ground, confused the warriors with the bouncing boulder and killed them all with his sword and spear.

That night, Medea sneaked away from the palace and went to Jason. "Darling," she told him, "my father means to kill the Argonauts. You must leave now and get the fleece. Take me with you, for he will soon come to know how I helped you yoke the bulls and kill the seed-grown men."

Jason readily obeyed and he and his men set out again on their quest. The crew rowed Jason and Medea up the river to a landing spot near the mighty oak. The lovers got out, and Medea brought Jason through the forest towards the gleaming Golden Fleece.

A twisting, terrible snake, the fleece's protector, shot out its tongue on seeing their approach. Its terrible head seemed to be floating towards the fearless Medea. She was a clever spell-caster, however, and she called out in her lovely, low voice to the god Sleep. Just as the snake was about to swallow Medea, Sleep dashed a misty drug in its eyes. The gapemouthed monster yawned and in a moment was asleep.

Jason scrambled up the oak and grabbed the Golden Fleece. He scrambled back down, and he and Medea, hand in hand, rushed back through the woods.

The fleece was so bright it lit up the lovers as if it were a sun. When the Argonauts saw the bright light approaching, they thought that Dawn had arrived.

*A twisting, terrible snake, the fleece's protector, shot out
its tongue on seeing their approach.*

"Hurry, men!" said Jason. "Let us be off!" The Argonauts rowed out on to the river and back to sea, narrowly evading King Aeetes' warships.

King Aeetes had sent his ships to chase down the Argonauts, and he demanded revenge on his daughter. Before the Argonauts had got very far, so many of Aeetes' ships blocked them, that they decided to give up Medea to Aeetes' sons.

At this, Medea grew angry, and Jason changed his mind, declaring that he would not give her up. And so Medea sent a message to Absyrtus, her brother, telling him she had been kidnapped, and wished to escape the Argonauts and that she would steal the Golden Fleece and return with him to their father. Absyrtus, believing her story, came to Medea from his ship. While he sat and talked to her, Jason came up from behind the innocent man and ruthlessly killed him.

This was a terrible crime: almighty Zeus was outraged by it and swore that the Argonauts would suffer for a long time before they reached home. The Argonauts learned of Zeus's wrath when the talking plank of the *Argo* told them of it.

They sailed for weeks and came within sight of the island of the dangerous Sirens, whose lovely voices drew sailors off their course and to their deaths on the rocky shores. They would have destroyed the *Argo* had not Orpheus plucked sweet music from his lyre, drowning out the voices of the Sirens. After the Sirens, the Argonauts sailed beyond the menacing Scylla and Charybdis, death traps to all ships, and towards the Wandering Rocks, steaming like lava. The Wandering Rocks would have tumbled up out of the sea and burned their ship had not lovely sea nymphs, at the command of Peleus' wife Thetis, taken hold of the ship and guided it safely past.

They next landed on the island of King Alcinous, where Jason and Medea married, spending their wedding night under the cover of the wondrous Golden Fleece. With gifts and treasures, the Argonauts set out once more.

They were soon home. The Argonauts again saw their dear families, their wives, their loving children.

As for Jason and Medea, their murder of Absyrtus haunted them the rest of their lives. Zeus resolved that even though they possessed the Golden Fleece and were able to bring about the death of the wicked King Pelias who had sent Jason on the quest, they were not to be happy. They ended their guilty lives far from either of their homelands.

Orpheus and Eurydice

Now let us hear the story of the great musician and singer Orpheus. A sad fate awaited this poet of the *Argo*. We know that when Orpheus sang to the tunes he played on his lyre even the muddy stones on the side of the road sat up and listened. The trees swayed in time to his music. He gave spirit to those things which have none and joy to those which have. If a man or a beast felt hot, eager anger, Orpheus' songs would soon soothe him.

Orpheus fell in love with Eurydice. They trembled with delight in each other's presence and their love gave Orpheus the joy that his music gave others. They were soon married.

It was during their honeymoon that a son of Apollo, Aristaeus, desiring Eurydice for his own, chased her. She, dashing away from the path to escape him, stepped on a snake, which bit her. She tumbled to the ground and cried for help. Aristaeus was frightened and ran away. Orpheus was terrified at her desperate call and came running to her.

But he was too late.

Orpheus cried. His beloved was dead! He wandered away, tears in his eyes. Even in his grief, however, Orpheus' lyre still played beautifully and his voice still melted the hearts of stones, as well as men's soft hearts, and his songs of sorrow made the gods weep. Zeus asked fleet-footed Hermes to go to the mortal. "Escort him alive down to Hades," commanded Zeus through his tears. "See if my brother Hades, lord of the dead, will return Eurydice to him."

Hermes took Orpheus by the hand and led the way across the seas to the secret entrance of the underworld. The terrible three-headed watchdog, Cerberus, hearing Orpheus' sweet music, lay down and sighed, and, without the faintest bark, allowed the god and his mortal guest to go past.

Orpheus sang his mournful story to the lord and queen of the underworld, Hades and Persephone.

Perhaps remembering her own sweet life above ground, Persephone had pity for Orpheus and persuaded her husband to return Eurydice's soul to the upper world, where she could live again with her beloved.

"Very well," said Hades. "You go on your way, back the way you came, and Eurydice will follow. But you must not look at her until she has passed out of the underworld. If you do, she will stay here with me. You may look at her all you like once you get her above."

Orpheus promised not to look. As the singer proceeded through the dark, dreary caves of the underworld, followed by Eurydice, he wanted to turn and see his wonderful wife. He resisted and resisted, but the way out was so long and so winding that he feared she might get lost.

Finally, he was so afraid that she had not been able to follow him that he slowly turned his head around to look. His eyes grew wide, and there he saw her, his dear Eurydice. He reached for her, to take her by the hand—and she began to fade and disappeared, leaving with Orpheus only the memory of her loving expression.

He cried out, for he was now back at the entrance to the underworld. Cerberus shoved him along, out of the way, with three snarling snouts. Orpheus turned again, hoping to be allowed to return and beg for Eurydice, but Hermes held him back, and Cerberus snarled.

Hermes led the grieving man home. Poor Orpheus' heart for music was gone, and thereafter he lived and died alone.

Chapter V
The Trojan War

WHEN THE goddess Eris, a notorious trouble-maker, was not invited to the marriage of Peleus and the sea nymph Thetis (this was before Peleus' time aboard the *Argo*), she created Strife. This Strife is the bad feeling that causes disputes, fights and wars.

Outside the gates of the wedding celebration, Eris etched upon a shiny golden apple the words: "To the Most Beautiful." She then tossed this apple out into a group of the grandest goddesses, who were, until this moment, enjoying the wedding.

The goddesses all grabbed for the apple, and it fell. In the scuffle for it, one of the goddesses kicked it, and it landed at the feet of Zeus.

"It's up to you, my dear," said Hera, Zeus's wife, "to decide to whom that apple belongs."

"Yes, Zeus," said Aphrodite.

"Please use your wisdom, Father, and decide the matter," said Athena, who had been born from Zeus's forehead.

Zeus made the wise decision to give the responsibility to Paris, a handsome young shepherd on Mount Ida, near Troy. The ladies agreed that they would submit themselves to the judgment of Paris.

Each goddess made her case to Paris for the apple, and each, in turn, offered him gifts if he should name her the Most Beautiful.

Queen Hera was first, and she told him, "If you choose me, you will have power and become the greatest king in the world."

Paris, one of the dozens of sons of King Priam of Troy, thought carefully about this offer.

Athena came to him next and told him, "What is power? What king is powerful next to a wise man who has more than the world in his own head? If you name me the Most Beautiful, I shall make you the wisest man in the world."

But then Aphrodite came to him and said, "Paris, handsome one, what are you thinking about? How could you want miserable power or the wisdom that makes you aware of your own smallness and shortness of life? What more could you want than beauty— the most beautiful mortal woman in the world? If you award me the apple, you shall have her."

"Power is good," he said, scratching his chin, "as is wisdom. But I agree that the love of a beautiful woman is best." He handed Aphrodite the apple.

The goddess of love was triumphant and her beautiful face beamed with satisfaction.

Hera and Athena on the other hand, were angry and immediately swore revenge on Paris and his homeland Troy.

Now the most beautiful woman in the world was

none other than Helen, wife of King Menelaus of
Sparta in Greece. Before she had married Menelaus,
dozens of princes and kings from the Grecian islands
and coastlands had gone to try to win her favor. To
prevent their fighting among themselves, Helen's
father asked them each to swear to uphold the rights
of whoever became her husband. When Menelaus
won her hand, all the competitors swore loyalty to
him should anyone try to take Helen away from him.
Aphrodite now brought Paris to Menelaus' homeland
and introduced him to Helen. Helen soon found
herself captivated by the stranger's handsome face
and charming words. As soon as Menelaus left the
palace, she and Paris sailed away to Troy.

It was this deed that brought on the Trojan War.
Menelaus and his brother Agamemnon called on
Helen's former suitors now to help regain Helen, as
they had promised to do. The spurned goddesses
Athena and Hera, angry with Paris for not having
given either of them the golden apple, of course took
the brothers' side.

Each of the suitors provided armies, and, under
Agamemnon's command, met to plan their strategy at
Aulis. While there, Agamemnon went out on a hunt.
He shot a deer with his bow and arrow, and cheered
his own masterful shot. "I am as fine a hunter as
Artemis!" he declared. Now Artemis, the goddess of
hunting, overheard this remark.

"No mortal man, even as great as Agamemnon,
may compare his abilities to mine!" she declared.

Artemis then waited for her chance for revenge.

When the Greeks were ready to sail, the winds would not come. The Greeks offered sacrifices. A priest came and told Agamemnon: "You have offended Artemis. Your fleet of ships will not have wind to sail until you sacrifice your oldest daughter, Iphigenia."

Agamemnon was distressed at this and cursed the foolish pride that had brought on his rash words. Hoping the goddess would forgive him, he prayed and offered her the best of the many deer he and his men had killed. But Artemis would not accept these substitutes. Agamemnon sadly sent messengers home to Argos to his wife, Clytemnestra. They asked her to send Iphigenia to Aulis, saying that Agamemnon wanted her to marry a warrior.

When Iphigenia arrived, Agamemnon explained to her his offense against the goddess and told her what Artemis had asked.

Iphigenia bowed and said, "You must kill me, father."

Weeping, the sorrowful Agamemnon sacrificed his lovely daughter.

Artemis was pacified, and she allowed the winds to return to Aulis. The Greek ships, at the cost of a terrible sacrifice, set out for Troy.

Achilles

The most famous and greatest warrior among the Greeks was Achilles, the son of Thetis and Peleus, the couple at whose wedding Strife was created.

Because Achilles was the son of a mortal—Peleus—he too would be mortal. In her concern over this, Thetis brought him as a baby to the River Styx in Hades and dipped him into its waters, being careful to keep hold of him lest he drown. Touched by these waters, forever after would Achilles' body be invulnerable—all but his heel and ankle by which his mother had grasped him.

Thetis then returned to live in the sea, and Peleus brought his son to be raised by the wise, immortal centaur, Cheiron, who lived in a mountain cave, and who had also taught Hercules. Achilles grew up eating the meat of lions, boars and bears to make him strong and honey to make him kindly and smooth-speaking. He learned to hunt, train horses and make medicines.

When Achilles was a young man, Odysseus and Achilles' best friend and cousin, Patroklos, came to him and asked him (even though he had not been a suitor for Helen's hand) to join the Greek expedition against the Trojans.

Achilles agreed and led a ship of countrymen to Troy and for nine years he and his mates fought the

Trojans and raided neighboring lands. It was the aftermath of one of these raids that caused a dispute between proud Achilles and stern Agamemnon.

Lord Agamemnon had captured a woman on a raid. This woman was the daughter of a priest of Apollo. The priest offered gold and treasures for her return, but Agamemnon would not give her back. Even when Apollo set plagues upon the Greeks Agamemnon stood aloof. It was not until Agamemnon's fellow officers, especially Achilles, insisted he return the woman that he did so. But, in turn, Agamemnon ordered that Achilles give him Briseis, the woman Achilles had captured.

This order brought on Achilles' fiery wrath. For a moment it seemed that Achilles would take his sword and kill Agamemnon, but the wise Athena invisibly came and told him not to do so. Instead Achilles answered, "If you take my woman, I shall not serve you but withdraw from all fighting. I swear that every Greek soldier will one day call to have me back, battling on their side. But I shall not, and you will remember this unfair act of yours and moan with sorrow in your heart. I shall not return to fight even when the Trojans have reached and set fire to one of our ships."

And so Achilles' terrible rage kept him and his crew from the fight; they would not join the Greeks in the following days' battles against the Trojans. The Greeks so missed Achilles, that after the long nine years away from their wives and children, many warriors wished to give up the war and sail away. It was only through goddess Athena's power that the men soon longed to fight again, preferring war to thoughts of home.

The fighting raged on each side, the gods allowing neither the Greeks nor the Trojans to win all the time. Angry arrows and bloodthirsty spears sped from the Trojans' bows and hands as they tried to defend their walled city. Piercing arrows and long spears shot through the air in return from the Greeks.

The Trojans were led by mighty Hector, the greatest and fiercest of King Priam's many sons. He did not resent Helen for this war; he resented his brother Paris.

Finding Paris within the walled city rather than on the battlefield, Hector scolded his brother and ordered him to return: "Our men are dying because of you, while you lie inside, kissing Helen."

"I am a lover, not a fighter," replied Paris. "But I shall return to the battlefield at once."

Hector went on to his own palace to find his wife, Andromache, and son Astyanax. How brightly Hector smiled upon his baby boy! Andromache took her husband's hand, and said, "O darling, you must not be so brave! If you keep challenging those Greeks, they will surely kill you, and by this you will leave me and your son alone. Be kind! Stay here within the walls! Do not bring grief to your child and me!"

"My lady," said Hector sadly, "such things worry me as well. But I am the commander of Troy's defenses, and so I must fight." After he said this he reached out to hold his son. But the baby cried out, frightened by the bobbing horsehair atop Hector's gleaming helmet. The mother and father laughed. Hector removed the helmet and placed it on the ground. He then took Astyanax and kissed him, and gave him back to his mother, who was crying. He kissed her as well and then picked up his helmet and went on his way, returning to the deadly battlefield.

Strife herself was overjoyed to see the clash of weapons again, and how Hector stormed out of Troy and through the ranks of Greeks, wounding many and killing more. He led the Trojans to the ramparts the Greeks had built before their ships, and with a tremendous boulder smashed through the high, heavy gates. Hector could not be stopped!

Patroklos, Achilles' truest friend, came to Achilles weeping, asking the greatest warrior to rejoin the fight. "You have too much pride," said Patroklos. "What good does your resentment against Agamemnon do? The Greeks are suffering disaster! Have you any feelings at all? I think Thetis and Peleus were not your parents; the stony cliffs and the cold dark sea are!"

Achilles was moved but would not yet rejoin the battle. Instead, he allowed Patroklos to wear his armor and thus make the Greeks and Trojans believe he, Achilles, had returned to fight.

"But do not try to fight the Trojans to their walls," warned Achilles. "Return to me before you do so."

Patroklos led the Greeks in pushing back the Trojans, but not before mighty Hector had set a Greek ship on fire. As the Trojans, feeling the tide of battle suddenly turn, retreated towards Troy, Patroklos was excited by his success; fury took over his mind, and he forgot Achilles' warning. The Trojans, near the city walls, suddenly turned on Patroklos and battled him; fearsome Hector then took away his life.

When Achilles heard the news about his friend, stormclouds gathered in his mind and heart. Immortal Thetis, Achilles' mother, heard his cries of pain and came to him.

"Achilles, my son," she said, "please listen. If you return to your country, you will rule over all of Phthia and live long and in quiet comfort, dying peacefully in old age. If you stay here in Troy, you will have glory as a warrior and decide the outcome—but you will die, unbent by years, in battle, mourned by all the Greeks."

"I will stay," said Achilles. "My life will be glorious— and so, too, perhaps, my death."

"This choice," said his mother, "I dreaded and yet expected." She then provided her son with new armor and a new shield, worked fine and gleaming by the god of fire, Hephaestus.

Achilles in his wrath went out onto the battlefield and slew many Trojans. When he met the greatest of them, Patroklos' killer, Hector, Achilles thirsted for that man's death. Poor Hector, great as he was, brave as he was, was frightened, running three times around the walled city before turning to face terrible Achilles. The men fought with swords and spears, and Achilles won the deadly contest. So powerful was Achilles' rage that he dragged Hector's lifeless body behind his team of horses. As Achilles rode around and around the walled city, Hector followed in the dust. This brutal act maddened the Trojans with grief.

After many days of this merciless treatment, Priam, Hector's father, went with the messenger god Hermes to Achilles and begged for the body of his son. Achilles gave up his punishment of Hector and returned the body, allowing Priam safe passage back to his city and a truce for the time Priam needed to hold Hector's funeral.

One day Achilles battled the Trojans all the way to the walls of their city. Apollo, the god of light and a patron of the Trojans, warned him away. "Beware, mortal Achilles," said Apollo. "Know that you must respect the laws of men and war. There is a time for peace even in war. Return to your camp."

Heedless even of a god, Achilles fought on. Atop the city walls, Paris aimed his bow at Achilles. "I will kill that raging Greek," he said, "though, somehow, he always seems to escape dark death."

Apollo, unseen by Paris, tipped the Trojan's bow and directed the flight of the death-dealing arrow into Achilles' vulnerable heel.

Achilles tumbled over, sprawled across the bloody earth, darkness misting his eyes.

Mighty Achilles was dead. His mates fought off the

*Apollo tipped the Trojan's bow and directed the flight of
the death-dealing arrow into Achilles' vulnerable heel.*

Trojans and rescued Achilles' body and brought it back to camp, where they held his glorious funeral.

The war was ten years old when the cleverest of the Greeks, Odysseus, came up with a trick to defeat the Trojans and end the war.

He prayed to the goddess Athena, and she instructed him to have the skillful Epeius build an enormous wooden horse, as big as a hill, with room inside to hold two dozen soldiers.

"You will hide yourself and other Greek heroes within it, while the rest of your forces burn their camp and sail away," said Athena. "The Trojans will bring the horse within their fort. This gift will be their downfall."

Odysseus thanked Athena and did as he was told. Epeius, a master ship-builder, understood the plan and on the shore constructed the horse out of sturdy lumber.

The Greeks set fire to their camp and got into their ships. Meanwhile, Odysseus, Menelaus and other Greek heroes climbed up a rope ladder into the wooden horse and Epeius himself went up last and closed the trap door.

The Trojans were joyous to see the Greek ships sail away into the Aegean Sea. On the other hand, the giant wooden horse the Greeks had left by the water troubled many Trojan leaders, including King Priam. They came down to the sea to inspect it. The words carved into its side awed many: "The Greeks on their journey home honor Athena with this gift of thanks."

Some Trojans cried out, "It is a trick! The Greeks are not our friends, and we should not trust them. Let us burn the horse or sink it in the sea."

King Priam did not listen to the skeptics, and ordered that the horse be brought within the city's walls.

That night, after the Trojans had finished their celebrating, and all was quiet, Odysseus and his men sneaked out of the wooden horse. The Greek ships had returned in the dark to the Trojan shore, and the sailors were ready and waiting on the beach for their signal.

One of Odysseus' soldiers lit a torch and waved it from the top of the city's walls. This was the signal. Others who had been hiding within the horse opened wide the city's tall doors.

Troy awoke to the shouts of fire and death. The Greeks invaded from within and without. King Priam and all his sons were killed. The entire city was burned and destroyed, its walls tumbling down. Aeneas was the lone Trojan hero to survive; he sailed away and established the great city of Rome.

Through the trick of the Trojan Horse, Menelaus recovered his wife Helen, Troy was wiped out, and the homesick Greek warriors finally were able to start on their way back across the sea.

Agamemnon soon returned to Argos, his homeland. His wife Clytemnestra, who, together with his cousin Aegisthus, had sworn revenge for his sacrifice of Iphigenia, greeted him and served him at his table. Then Clytemnestra screamed, "You killed our daughter, and now I kill you!" And Clytemnestra and Aegisthus struck him with axes.

Agamemnon's children, Electra and Orestes, came upon this murder and were horrified. Electra spoke to her brother's teacher, and begged the man to take Orestes out of the country. She thought that her mother would kill the boy, who would surely want to avenge his father's murder.

And so Orestes left the country with his teacher, and Electra remained, living in the royal palace with her murderous mother and the new king, Aegisthus. Electra hated her mother and her mother's new husband. Whenever Electra had the chance, she would insult Clytemnestra for her outrageous deed: "You are a murderess! What is worse than killing one's husband?"

Her mother would then answer her: "Killing one's child is worse! He killed my daughter—your sister! Why do you worship your father's memory and not Iphigenia's?"

"I worship the memory of both. Iphigenia agreed to her own death, but my father did not!"

Many years later Orestes returned to Argos to avenge his father's murder. Electra and he plotted secretly their terrible deed of revenge. And then one afternoon, with wicked shouts of glee, they killed Clytemnestra and Aegisthus. Death upon death had come to this cursed family.

Another Greek hero who returned home from the war was Odysseus. The next chapter is devoted to his adventures.

Chapter VI
The Odyssey

ODYSSEUS, THE wise warrior from the rocky island of Ithaca, began his adventurous journey home after the sack of Troy. His experiences took him all over the world, across the seas to strange countries and even to the land of the dead, before he again saw his patient wife Penelope and son Telemachos. The goddess of wisdom Athena admired him and protected him, or he, too, certainly would have perished.

Soon after Odysseus and his men sailed from Troy, they landed and raided the Kikonians of Thrace. Maron, a Kikonian priest of the god Apollo, in thanks for being spared his life, gave Odysseus casks of divine wine, a gift that would later save Odysseus' life. Greedy with the riches they found in Thrace, many of Odysseus' men set sail too late and died battling the neighbors of the Kikonians.

Odysseus and the remaining ships next landed far away, desperate for food and water, on the island of the Lotus-eaters. After the sailors had hunted for food and eaten, curious Odysseus wanted to know what kind of people lived there. He sent three men to go up from the smooth, quiet shore and discover the dwellers nearby.

After several hours with no sign from his faithful scouts, Odysseus worried that the natives must have killed them. So, arming himself and a few other men, Odysseus set out to look for them. The island was beautiful. The weather was mild, warm but not hot, and the breeze was gentle.

They came to a simple hut and Odysseus called out to whoever was inside, "We are Greek warriors returning home from Troy. Have you see my men?"

No one answered. Odysseus heard a contented moaning, however, so he looked inside. There were his men and several dreamy-looking natives, all sitting around a large basket of sweet-smelling fruit. They looked blissful, with neither wants nor desires. Every few moments they would reach for the sweet, fragrant fruit of the lotus. These Lotus-eaters had given themselves entirely to the dumb forgetfulness that the lotus brought to their minds.

"Come along now," said Odysseus to his men. "We must go back to the ship and sail for home. It has been many years since we have seen our wives, our families, our homes."

One of Odysseus' men looked up with a smile and mumbled, "Lotus, captain."

Odysseus took a piece and lifted it to his nose. The lotus fruit was fragrant and fresh and filled Odysseus' head with forgetfulness. Odysseus shook his head and made himself drop the fruit, or he too would have been content never to reach home.

"It is wrong," said Odysseus, "to forget your homeland. You must come with me, my men."

"I prefer to stay here," said each of his lotus-eating sailors.

Odysseus and his armed men now grabbed hold of the dreamy-eyed sailors and dragged them out of the hut. Those men were pitiful, moaning like babies torn from the breast. Odysseus and his men tied them up and carried them back down to the shore, leaving the natives to their forgetful, blissful ways. It took several days of rowing on the ocean before Odysseus' lotus-eating sailors forgot their craving for the honey-sweet fruit and once more remembered their dear home.

Next they landed on a bountiful, hilly island, the home of the brutal, lawless Cyclopes. The Cyclopes were giants with a single, gloomy eye in the middle of their foreheads. They wore shaggy beards and lived apart from gods and men.

At first, Odysseus and his men were overjoyed to see the gigantic fruit that swung from the trees and vines in the land of the Cyclopes. They ate and drank to their hearts' content before Odysseus and eight of his men wandered further into the land. They brought with them a present of mind-numbing wine, the gift to them from Maron, the Kikonian priest of Apollo. They followed a trail into a deep cave carved out of a mountainside. Within the cave were large empty pens for sheep and tremendous hanging cheeses. Odysseus and his men knew nothing of the ways of the rude Cyclopes and so helped themselves to a tiny portion of one cheese and waited for the return of the cave dweller and his sheep.

Then the ground shuddered as giant sheep hurried into the cave and into their pens. It was when the Cyclops named Polyphemos, a son of the sea god Poseidon, entered the cave that the men, not just the earth, shuddered. Polyphemos was terrible to look at, draped as he was in a beast's skin, his beard and hair long and wild—and his single eye bulging. The monster lifted a rock the size of a cliff and set it in the mouth of the cave, locking out all those beyond, and shutting in all those within.

It was only after several moments that the Cyclops, while making his fire for dinner, noticed the strangers. He knew no manners and, instead of greeting his guests, said loudly, "What are you doing here?"

"We are sailors, and our ships," said Odysseus, thinking up a lie, "were wrecked on this island's rocky shores."

"Indeed," said Polyphemos. "How lucky for me." He suddenly snatched up two of Odysseus' men, and crunched them in his mouth as if they were two grapes.

The remaining men were terrified, but Odysseus, always thinking, stepped out and addressed the monster. "Please sir, after that meal you must be thirsty. When our ships were destroyed, we managed to save this cask of wine. We offer it to you, and hope that you will remember your manners and offer a gift in return." Now, the wine in the cask was so intoxicating that even the gods and goddesses mixed it with several parts of water.

"What are you doing here?" said the Cyclops.

The Cyclops lifted the cask and drank it long and deep. "Ah!" He smacked his moist lips and said to Odysseus, "Very good. I will offer you a guest gift, friend. What is your name?"

Odysseus thought a moment and answered, "Noman!"

"As my present to you, Noman, I shall eat you last!" The Cyclops laughed and snatched up two more of Odysseus' mighty warriors. He ate them as he had eaten the first two. Then, overpowered by the potent wine, he lay down to sleep.

The remaining men, trembling with fear, mourned for their friends who had been eaten. Odysseus wept for a time, but then he sat down and thought. At last he had a plan to rescue himself and the others. It would do no good to slay the giant, for they would never be able to lift the rock from the cave's entrance. Odysseus directed his men to pick up a broken wooden staff, as tall as a tree, with which Polyphemos shepherded his flocks. They sharpened it with their axes and then lay one end of the log in the fire that the Cyclops had lit, and when the fire caught the wood, they rolled the blackening point and hardened it.

Odysseus and his men hoisted the log and rushed towards the slumbering Cyclops. They jabbed the burning spear into the monster's eye, which sizzled and spit, and twisted the point.

The giant, groaning in agony, reached out here and there for Odysseus and his men, but they had run and safely found a corner where Polyphemos' terrible hands could not reach.

His shouts roused the Cyclopes who lived on the other side of the mountain.

They came to his entry way and shouted:

"What is it, Polyphemos? Why are you screaming? Did somebody hurt you?"

"Noman!" said Polyphemos.

"Oh, then," said the other Cyclopes, "if no man has hurt you, why are you bothering us?" They returned to their own caves.

When it was morning, Polyphemos' sheep wailed, like babies, to be allowed to go out to graze on the rich, lush meadows. Odysseus and his men, clever schemers, were clutching the wool underneath the giant sheep's bellies, hoping to ride out past the Cyclops. Polyphemos lifted the rocky cliff from the cave's entrance and told his sheep, lovingly running his hands over their backs, "You feel sorry for me, don't you? You are walking slowly today because you are sad that your master is now blind."

When the sheep reached the gentle meadows, Odysseus and his men let go their hold of the wool and tumbled to the grass. Then they herded several of the sheep and ran down the hillside towards the safe cove where their ships lay.

Polyphemos by now had realized the men had escaped, and he was in a rage, calling out at them, "Come back! Let me give you the gift you deserve!"

Odysseus could not resist taunting the rude Cyclops, and he called out to him, "You wicked, beastly monster. Know that it was Odysseus who blinded you!"

Polyphemos felt his dark way along and climbed a mountain and broke off the top of it. While Odysseus and his men sailed away, Polyphemos heaved that mountaintop in the direction of Odysseus' voice. The rocky peak barely missed Odysseus' ship's stern, and in the tall wave the splashing mountaintop created, the ships bounded forward on the sea, away from the island of the one-eyed Cyclopes.

They then sailed to Aiolia, where lived Aiolos, the keeper of all the winds. Aiolos was fond of Odysseus and wanted him to reach his home on rocky Ithaca. He gave the captain a bag of winds; the only wind Aiolos left out, which he sent after them to sweep them along home, was the west wind. On and on the ships sailed. But, just within sight of their homeland Ithaca, Odysseus' men grew curious to see what treasures their captain had in the bag from Aiolos, and opened it up; the terrible winds tossed their ships clear back to Aiolia. The weary men went back to Aiolos' palace, and Aiolos was angry and disappointed to see them: "That Cyclops Polyphemos must have cursed you to his father Poseidon. The sea god bears a grudge against you, and I cannot help you. Now leave my island before Poseidon punishes me in turn."

After this came a total absence of wind. For six days the ships had to be rowed by the sailors. This was exhausting work. At the end of six days the weary fleet landed on a strange island, and decided to rest there. While the rest of his fleet put into a deep bay,

Odysseus cautiously kept his own ship moored in open waters. What happened next showed that his instincts had been correct: a party of sailors from the fleet went inland to look for food and met with a tribe called the Laistrygones, who, being the fiercest of cannibals, tore them to pieces and ate them on the spot. This brought the entire tribe to the place where the fleet was resting in the deep bay. Swiftly and violently, Odysseus' entire fleet was demolished and devoured by the Laistrygones—all save his own ship and crew. As they sailed away from the island, Odysseus and his men mourned the sudden loss of so many of their friends.

Their next adventure was on the island called Aiaia, home of the enchanting immortal witch Circe. Several of Odysseus' men went to her, and she fed them, but with her magic turned them into swine. The messenger god Hermes flew down to Odysseus, giving him a magic charm and guidance on how to reverse Circe's witchcraft. Odysseus then tricked her with the charm and forced her to turn his snorting sailors back into men. She was happy to do so; what's more, she became a kindly hostess. Odysseus and his men lived with Circe for a year, comfortable and happy, almost forgetting their homeland. Odysseus then asked Circe for news of his home, his wife Penelope and son Telemachos, and Circe told him the person to ask was the seer Teiresias. He knew the past, present and future and would tell them all to Odysseus, as well as how to return home. "But I must warn

you, dear Odysseus," said Circe, "you must travel into
the underworld, Hades' land of the dead, to find him."

Odysseus had never found an easy way to get
home, but this was surely the hardest journey yet. His
men sailed to the entrance of Hades, and Odysseus
went down into the underworld, where he saw sights
few living mortals see. He gave a bloody drink to the
spirit of Teiresias, and the seer looked into the future
for him, warning him of dangers and of all to come.
Next Odysseus spoke with his tearful mother, Antikleia, who had died with sorrow because of his
absence. When he tried to clasp her, she was like
vapor and his arms passed through her. He spoke
then to the great warriors of the Trojan War, his slain
comrades Agamemnon and Achilles. Soon satisfied
with his gloomy adventure, Odysseus returned with
his men to Circe's island, where she gave him further
warnings about the way home.

"As did Jason and the Argonauts, you will sail past
the rocky island of the Sirens," said Circe. "They sing
divinely, but do not let your men listen to them, or
your ship will be lured to its destruction on their
shores. If you want to hear their heavenly songs,
block your men's ears with wax and have yourself
tied to the mast.

"After you pass the Sirens, you will reach Scylla
and Charybdis. The passage between these is so
narrow," explained Circe, "the cliffs on either side
cast shadows across it all day long. In a cave, far up
one sheer cliff, lives Scylla, a horrible long-necked

beast who has six heads with voices like those of whimpering puppies; but those deceitful mouths hold brutal, sharp teeth like knives, and when she flashes out her neck she plucks sailors from the boat just as she fishes the sea below for dolphins and sharks. No ship can pass by her cave without losing six of its men.

"On the left side," continued Circe, "is Charybdis, which swallows ships whole, sucking them down and down to the bottom of the sea. Once a ship enters the whirling funnel of Charybdis, then hope is gone and all will perish. Three times a day does Charybdis swallow and spew. Perhaps you will be lucky and pass over the whirlpool while Charybdis is calm; but do not risk this. I advise you, dear Odysseus, to steer your ship closer to Scylla and lose six of your worthy men rather than risk destroying your entire ship in the churning, whirling Charybdis. You will know where Charybdis is by the lush fig tree that clings to the jagged cliff above it."

Odysseus replied: "We will sail under the cliffs, and I will stand ready at the prow with my spears waiting for Scylla."

"My good Odysseus, you still do not understand. She is an immortal beast and will take your men whether you try to fight her or not. No, your best effort will be to encourage your men to keep rowing. If they panic and your ship stalls in the waters below the cliff, Scylla will enjoy a second meal."

Last of all, she told him that when he reached

Thrinakia that he and his sailors were not to eat the
cattle of the sun god Helios. "No matter how hungry
you are, you must not allow the cattle to be touched,
or your weary men will never reach home," said Circe.

Odysseus thanked Circe and set out on the seas.

As they approached the Sirens, Odysseus deafened
the men by putting wax in their ears; then he had
them tie him to the mast. Listening to the delicious
voices of the Sirens, Odysseus was overcome with
joy. He pleaded with his men to bring him to the
Sirens' rocky shores, but fortunately they could not
hear him, and rowed on, keeping the ship safe.
Farther along, Odysseus was released from the mast,
the Sirens' singing still sweet in his memory.

As they approached the passage between Scylla
and Charybdis, Odysseus remembered Circe's warnings. He hoped even so to avoid Scylla's menace. He
stood on the prow and shouted at his men to row
hard. He peered and peered, searching out the cliffs
for the snake-necked killer. They heard a rush of
water and looked off to their left. There they saw
Charybdis sweeping all the ocean around it into a
terrible whirl. "Avoid the swirling waters, my men,"
ordered Odysseus.

Charybdis suddenly sucked down the waters and
the men could see the bottom of the sea. Charybdis
then spewed the water in a frightening explosion; the
men shouted. In the next moment Odysseus turned in
his boat and saw six of his crew rising above him,
grasped as prey and reeled away by terrible Scylla.

"Odysseus," the men called to him, "save us!"

Odysseus could do nothing as Scylla, at the entrance to her cave, devoured them; the remaining men pulled hard on their oars. They got away, weeping for their friends.

Odysseus and his men soon landed on Thrinakia, the home of Helios. While their own food lasted they were happy to resist the temptation of the sun god's marvelous herds of cattle. But as the days went on, with no wind to carry them on their way, the men became hungry and desperate. One afternoon, while Odysseus slept, the men killed, roasted and ate one of Helios' cattle. Odysseus prayed for forgiveness, but the gods did not show mercy. As Odysseus and his men sailed away with the wind, almighty Zeus, furious with their disrespect, destroyed Odysseus' ship and all the members of its crew—all but Odysseus.

Odysseus, alone, had to make a return journey on a raft between Scylla and Charybis. This time he chose to take his chances with the deadly whirlpool. At the moment Charybdis pulled his puny raft into its sucking waters, Odysseus leapt and grabbed hold of a branch on the fig tree about which Circe had told him, and there he remained, for many hours, hanging like a bat, until Charybdis spit out the raft once more. Odysseus dropped near the raft, and Zeus, seeing the man's plight, blinded Scylla's eyes until Odysseus paddled past her cavernous perch.

The sea nymph Calypso lived on an island, Ogygia, far across the ocean from any god or man. It was a surprise to her when she discovered the dying warrior Odysseus floating on a piece of timber on the waves. The long-haired nymph nursed the mortal back to health, sharing her food and her home with him. But as time passed, he would sit on the seashore day after day, weeping and remembering his family. He had been gone so very long from them all!

He had been with delightful Calypso seven years when the gods on Mount Olympos decided that the nymph should send poor Odysseus on his way. Hermes, the messenger of the gods, flew across the waters and arrived at Calypso's warm, well-stocked cave.

"Zeus, the king of the gods, has ordered that Odysseus be sent home, lovely Calypso," said Hermes.

"What! After I rescued him, after Zeus's thunderbolts destroyed his ship, now you want to take him from me?"

Hermes let angry Calypso have her say, and then he repeated his message. She nodded, because the gods and nymphs must all obey the word of Zeus.

After Hermes flew away, Calypso walked out to the shore and tapped weeping Odysseus on his shoulder. "Come with me," she said.

He followed and they ate. He ate mortal food and she the food of gods, nectar and ambrosia. Gorgeous Calypso now asked, "My mortal man, are you so sure you want to go home? If you stay with me I will make you immortal. Why is it you want to leave me? Could your mortal wife be my rival in beauty?"

Odysseus did not want to anger the nymph and answered: "Never could Penelope be as beautiful as you, for your beauty is timeless, everlasting. But I am mortal and miss my mortal life. My dear father and my baby son who has grown into a man have spent long years missing me. You saved my life, dear one, and yet now I wish to return home."

"Very well," said Calypso sadly, "As you wish."

The next morning, Calypso gave Odysseus everything he needed to make a raft. After five days he had completed it. On the sixth day she gave him many gifts and sent him on his way, blowing a steady breeze behind him to ease his voyage.

On this raft Odysseus made his way to the island of Scheria, home of the Phaiakians; there, a princess named Nausicaa discovered the sea-grimed sailor, cleaned him and fed him and introduced him to her parents, the king and queen. Odysseus told his long, sad, amazing story to his kind hosts, and they wept and invited him to marry their charming daughter.

"Thank you," said Odysseus, "but my lone desire is to return home."

The king's sailors rowed Odysseus home to Ithaca with many treasures. Odysseus was asleep when they landed, and they unloaded him and his possessions and rowed towards home, which, alas, they would never reach. Poseidon remained resentful of the injury Odysseus had caused his son Polyphemos the Cyclops, and so he punished Odysseus' rescuers by turning their boat to stone.

When Odysseus awoke, Athena had covered Ithaca with such a fog that he did not recognize his homeland. She appeared to him as a young boy, and he told her an incredible lie as to who he was and from where he had come. Athena laughed at him, and revealed to him now who she was, where he was and how a hundred threatening suitors would try to kill him if he returned to his palace. She then made him seem an old man and dressed him in rags, so that he could test the loyalty of his family and friends.

Keeping himself in disguise he found that his swineherd, Eumaios, reverenced Odysseus' memory, and treated kindly all strangers. Eumaios served the beggarly-seeming man food in his shelter and told him of the savage, rude suitors; of Odysseus' poor father Laertes, grieving and lonely on his farm, far from the city; of forlorn Penelope, awaiting Odysseus' return; and of Telemachos, Odysseus' brave son, who had traveled far and wide to hear any news of Odysseus.

Hearing of all this made Odysseus eager for revenge on the suitors, but Athena tempered his anger and made him await the return of Telemachos. Telemachos had escaped the death the suitors plotted for him and now came to see the swineherd. When Odysseus saw the handsome, sturdy young man he had known only as a baby, he nearly wept. Telemachos asked Eumaios about the stranger, and the swineherd told him about the old man.

Telemachos asked Eumaios to go to Laertes, Telemachos' grandfather, and to his mother, Penelope, with the news of his return. After Eumaios left the hut, Athena restored Odysseus' true form, and Telemachos was amazed.

"Are you a god?" he asked Odysseus.

"Not a god," said the man, "but your father."

They clasped, and Odysseus was overcome by tender weeping. They then planned for the suitors' destruction, and how Odysseus would enter the palace hall as a beggar, while Telemachos removed all the weapons from the hall. They went to town separately.

The suitors were disappointed to see Telemachos still alive, but Penelope was delighted to see her son. She asked him, touching his shoulder, "And have you heard news of your father?"

"No," said Telemachos, lying to his mother at Odysseus' request; for his father wanted to test each person's loyalty in turn.

"I thought you would not," said Penelope, who now lost hope of ever seeing her dear husband again.

Meanwhile, Odysseus' return to the palace as a beggar showed him the outrages committed by the suitors. In his disguise, whereby Athena again made him seem an older man, he claimed knowledge of Odysseus' return, and for this they made fun of him. "You lying scoundrel," they said. "You tell Penelope stories so that she'll give you a piece of bread and the corner of a hallway to sleep in."

"And you," returned Odysseus, "disrespect the laws

of hospitality, treating a poor old beggar with rudeness and a kind hostess with contempt, eating her out of house and home."

"What!" cried one of the suitors. "Talk to us like that!" And he hurled a stool at Odysseus. It struck him on the shoulder and tumbled away. Telemachos came forward in the hall and scolded the suitors for their behavior. Penelope, soon after, came from her elegant room, as beautiful as she had ever been. The suitors marveled at her dazzling face and hair, further angering Odysseus.

Beautiful Penelope announced, "We will have a contest. The man who is able to string my long-lost—and, alas, no doubt long-dead—husband's bow and shoot an arrow through a row of twelve axes shall have my hand in marriage." She then turned away and returned to her room.

Telemachos saw an opportunity for his father's revenge in this contest and set up the wood-handled axes in a long row, their long handles crossing each other and forming an alley of sharp curved blades. Only the strongest arms and hands could string such a large, strong bow; and only the surest archer could possibly guide his arrow through such a passage.

Each suitor tried to string the bow, and each suitor failed. When they had stopped to rest, angry with their failure, beggar-like Odysseus asked if he might have a try.

"Never!" cried a suitor. "Imagine a beast like you wedding a princess like she!"

"Why are you frightened now of a humble old man?" asked Telemachos.

The other suitors shouted that the beggar ought to be allowed a try, and Odysseus came over and sat down on a stool and picked up the bow. He looked it over, and then, like a musician stringing his instrument, easily pulled the bowstring over the tips of the bow and then plucked on the taut string. He picked up an arrow and notched it in the bowstring, and then let the arrow fly. It passed through the row of axes in an instant, perfectly.

Suddenly the suitors were in a panic, sensing something strange had come to pass.

Odysseus now announced his identity: "You mongrel dogs thought Odysseus would never return! But I have, and for your crimes against me and my family you all shall die!" Athena instantly restored to him his younger, stronger body.

Telemachos and Odysseus now began their terrible slaughter, killing every single suitor, spilling blood across the floor. When their merciless deed was done, and they had washed down the tables and floors and carried out the bodies, Odysseus went upstairs to see his wife and announce his identity to her.

"I have returned to you, dear Penelope," he said, "I am Odysseus."

She did not smile, she did not rush to him. She sat down and looked at him, wondering. For a moment she would recognize him, and then not. Finally, Odysseus became angry. "Why don't you come to me!"

"It has been so long," she said. "I am not yet sure. For tonight, I will have the servants move the bed Odysseus made for us out into the hallway, where you may sleep."

"My bed!" cried Odysseus, "in the hallway! That is not possible. I carved one of its posts from a living tree, around which I built that room!"

"Yes!" laughed Penelope, rushing to him. For she had tricked Odysseus into revealing a secret only he himself could know!

They were delighted, and they talked away the long night, telling each other their stories, happy to be together once more.

In the morning, Odysseus set out to find his father and tell him of his return. Laertes, who had grieved for his son and then for his wife, Antikleia, who had long since died of heartbreak for Odysseus, was overjoyed.

Odysseus had regained his kingdom, his son, his wife, and his father, thus ending his odyssey.